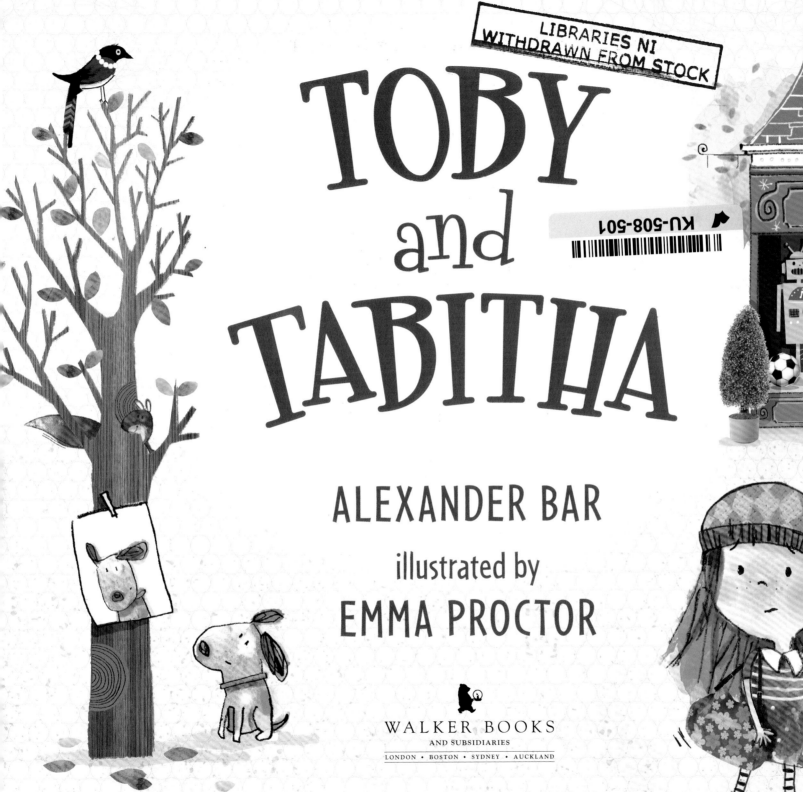

TOBY and TABITHA

ALEXANDER BAR

illustrated by
EMMA PROCTOR

WALKER BOOKS
AND SUBSIDIARIES

LONDON · BOSTON · SYDNEY · AUCKLAND

Lucy loved helping Grandpa in his shop.

She'd go there as often as she possibly could.

And every time she walked up to the door,

Grandpa would greet her with his huge, Grandpa smile.

"Welcome back to Animal Palace!" he'd say.

"The GREATEST pet shop in the whole universe!"

Lucy had not been to the whole universe,

but she did know that Animal Palace was,

without a feather of a doubt,

the BEST-SHOP-EVER!

Animal Palace was FULL of puppies and rabbits and kittens that hopped ...
gerbils and budgies and snakes that bopped!

And a chatterbox parrot that squawked,

Who's a pretty boy then?

Even to girls.

Lucy petted and played with all
the animals all day long as they
chirp-chirped and bow-wowed,
squeak-squeaked and m e - o w e d...

But for Lucy, the BEST thing about
the best shop ever was two teeny,
tiny tortoises called Toby and Tabitha,
who were tucked away in a little corner.

Toby and Tabitha didn't do anything. Except sleep.

And sleep.

AND SLEEP!

"There's more life in my old socks!" Grandpa would say.
But Lucy knew something about Toby and Tabitha that
no one else in the whole universe knew. Not *even* Grandpa...

When the evening drew in
and the shop was sleepy,
Lucy would go to that little corner,
to hum a hum and gently sing,

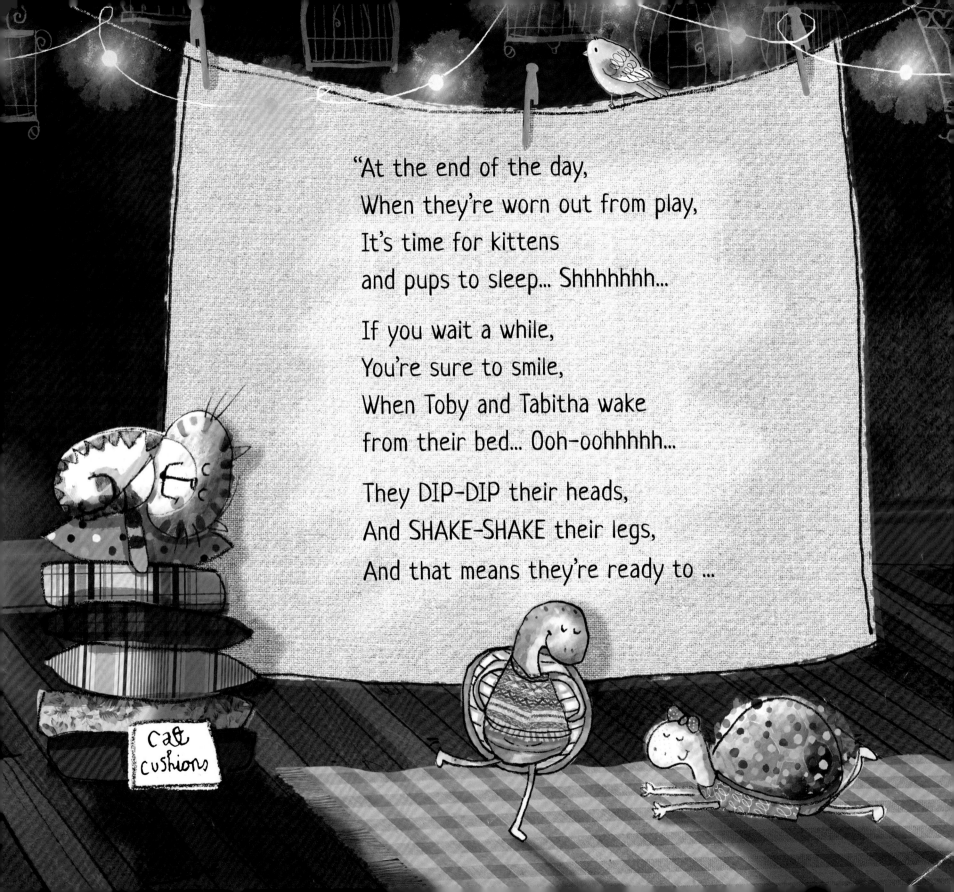

"At the end of the day,
When they're worn out from play,
It's time for kittens
and pups to sleep... Shhhhhhh...

If you wait a while,
You're sure to smile,
When Toby and Tabitha wake
from their bed... Ooh-oohhhhh...

They DIP-DIP their heads,
And SHAKE-SHAKE their legs,
And that means they're ready to ...

cat
cushions

That's right, DANCE!

With a TAPPITY TAP ...

and a RAT A TAT TAT ...

bet you've never seen tortoises
move quite like THAT!"

Lucy loved nothing more than to watch Toby and Tabitha twirling and whirling together, lighting up the room like two movie stars.

the "Bugsy Malone",

They did the "Walla Walla Boom Boom",

the "Lift and Shake" and the "Give Your Dog a Bone".

And what about Lucy? She didn't have a partner for those dances so she made up her own dance: "Tea for One".

And as long as Lucy had Toby and Tabitha, "Tea for One" would do just fine.

One afternoon Lucy
arrived at the shop,
just like she always did.

But something felt wrong.

**Where's
Tabitha?!**

Lucy cried out so loudly
that it made Grandpa jump
and everyone else in the shop
stand very still. Even
the happy, chatty parrot.

Lucy looked at Toby, all alone...
What would happen when he woke up
and Tabitha wasn't there?

"He was a lovely little boy..." Grandpa explained. He couldn't understand why Lucy was so upset. "I'm sure Tabitha will be very happy."

Lucy sobbed, "It's all my fault..." If only she'd shared her secret.

Suddenly, a small voice behind her said,

"Excuse me, but I forgot to ask: what do tortoises like to *do*?"

"TABITHA!" beamed Lucy, with a huge, Grandpa-wide smile.

"Do *you* know what tortoises like to do?" asked the boy.

Lucy thought for a moment before saying "I can show you..."

CHAMP
food

So, Lucy hummed a hum
and gently sang...

Toby stretched out
his hand. Tabitha took it.
And they danced like they
had never danced before.

In sharing her secret, Lucy had made a friend.
And his name was Jack. "Toby and Tabitha should stay together,
right here," Jack said.
"Today, tomorrow and every day after," Lucy agreed.
"But ... can I visit?" asked Jack.
"Every day..." Lucy said shyly.

So Jack returned Tabitha.
And for the first time ever,
Lucy wasn't dancing alone,
and "Tea for One" became
"Tea for Two" and a party ...

YOU ARE INVITED TO

tea for Two

RSVP
Animal Palace